Animals Need Water

Written by Josephine Selwyn

Picture Dictionary

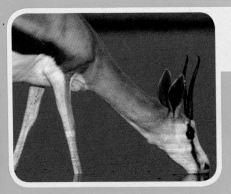

antelope

elephant

giraffe

lion

rhinoceros

zebra

This lion is drinking.
It needs water to live.

This rhinoceros is drinking. It needs water to live.

horn

This zebra is drinking.
It needs water to live.

hoof

This elephant is drinking.
It needs water to live.

This antelope is drinking.
It needs water to live.

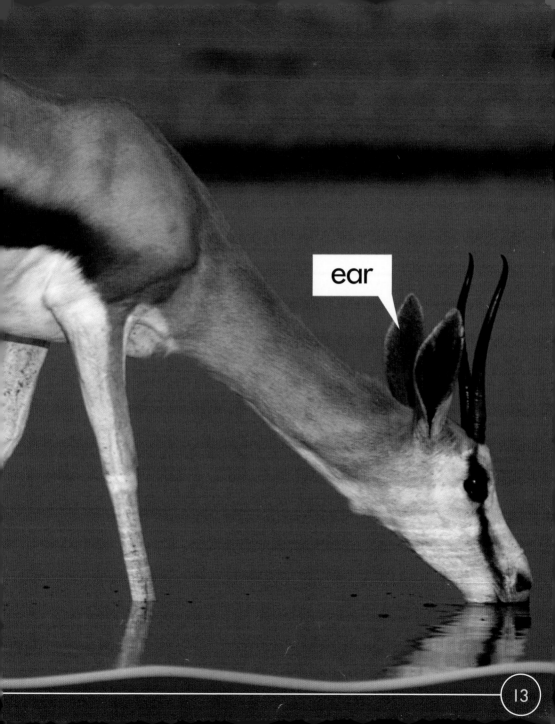

This giraffe is drinking.
It needs water to live.

neck

Activity Page

Copy the picture. Use the words in the book to label the parts.

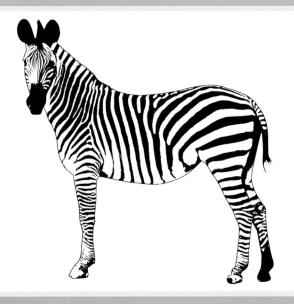

Do you know the dictionary words?